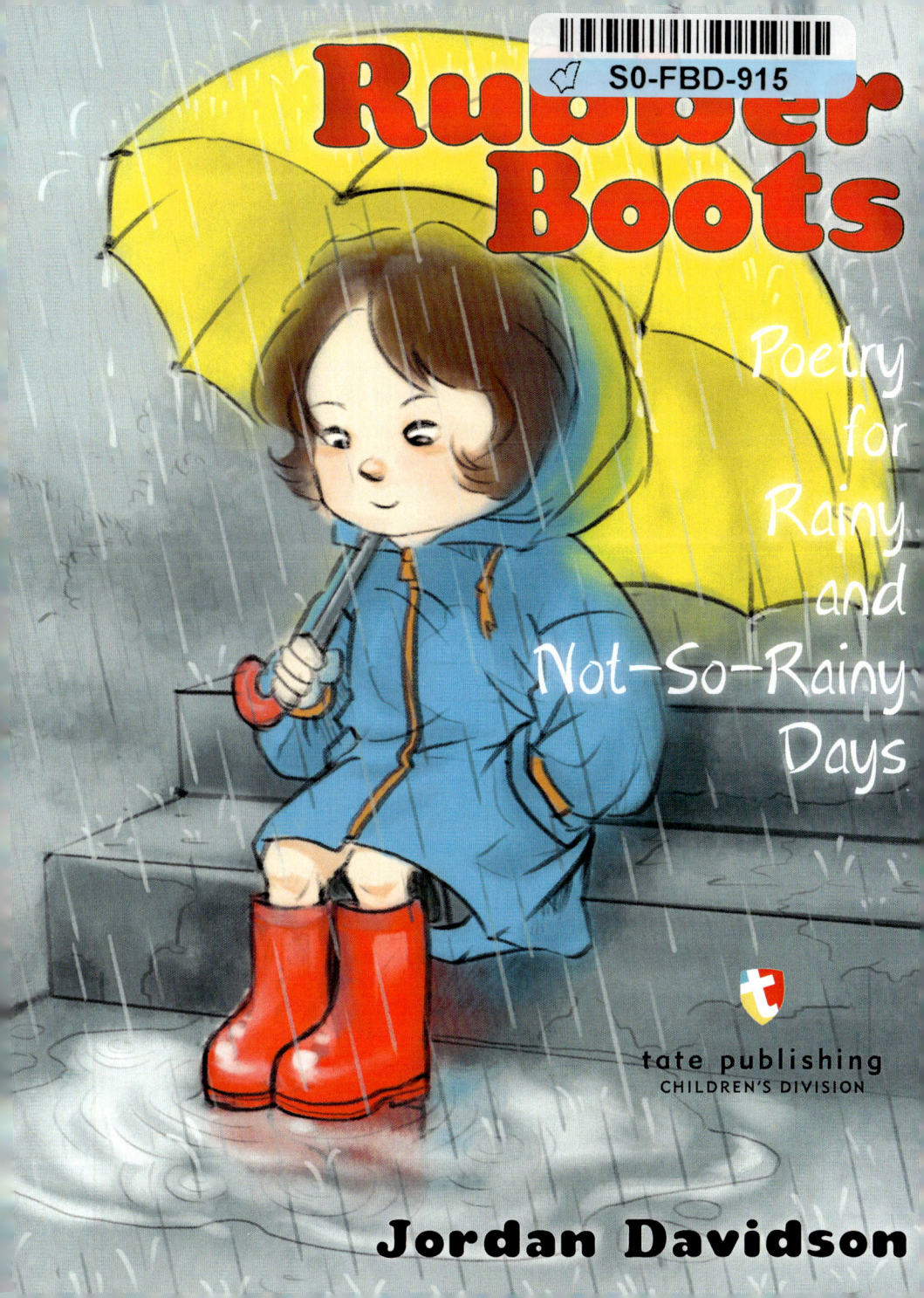

Rubber Boots: Poetry for Rainy and Not-So-Rainy Days
Copyright © 2014 by Jordan Davidson. All rights reserved.

This title is also available as a Tate Out Loud product. Visit www.tatepublishing.com for more information.

No part of this publication may be reproduced, stored in a retrieval system or transmitted in any way by any means, electronic, mechanical, photocopy, recording or otherwise without the prior permission of the author except as provided by USA copyright law.

The opinions expressed by the author are not necessarily those of Tate Publishing, LLC.

Published by Tate Publishing & Enterprises, LLC
127 E. Trade Center Terrace | Mustang, Oklahoma 73064 USA
1.888.361.9473 | www.tatepublishing.com

Tate Publishing is committed to excellence in the publishing industry. The company reflects the philosophy established by the founders, based on Psalm 68:11,
"The Lord gave the word and great was the company of those who published it."

Book design copyright © 2014 by Tate Publishing, LLC. All rights reserved.
Cover and interior design by James Mensidor
Illustrations by Madeleine ma Boone

Published in the United States of America

ISBN: 978-1-63122-575-8
Juvenile Nonfiction / Poetry / General
14.02.20

Dedication

This book is dedicated to Baby D.

Acknowledgments

Mom, thank you for your help throughout this whole process.

Part I: Spring Collection

Heaven

Heaven should be a wonderful place,
Where you and I shall see a new face;
Where poppies and daisies grow everywhere,
And all that we breathe is mountain air.
Where streets are of gold,
And we will not be cold.
Where questions are asked;
I hope Jesus can multitask.
Where people and angels are friends,
And where there are no dead ends.
Where there are libraries full of books,
Of how to clean, play music, or cook.
Where the gates are made of gems;
All because of Him.
Just think, I get to go there and I get to hear Him say "Come near and let me show you my ways, so they will shine clear."

Blooming Flowers

When the sun rises in the East,
All the flowers turn to look.
They open up their delicate petals,
Trying to get a sprinkle of sunlight.
The leaves on the stem strengthen,
Trying to catch a glimmer of the gold dust.
Once the flower is in full bloom,
It shines and shimmers,
Showing everything that is a miraculous sight.

Waterfall

Rushing down,
In no hurry, though.
A peaceful stream runs atop.
The sound is like thunder,
Above a mountain.
The jagged rocks look down,
Like eyes,
Peeking out at the sunshine.
A sparkling pool lies at the bottom,
Still as glass.

Rubber Boots

Whenever it is a rainy day,
I always go outside and play.
I put on my coat and my hat,
And grab my rubber boots off the mat.
Off I go into the world beyond,
Of which I have always been fond.
I jump in puddles with a big splash,
My boots are muddy in a flash.
With water dripping down my coat,
I skip over an imaginary moat.
My body is wet from head to toe,
I think that I should really go.
I take off my coat and my hat,
And wipe my rubber boots on the mat.
My rainy day has come to an end,
I hope to use my rubber boots again.

Weeping Willow

Weeping willow, why do you cry?
You are almost as tall as the sky.
Your trunk stands so sturdy and strong,
Your branches sway to the wind's sorrowful song.
Forever you will stand,
Rooted in the ground.
Forever you will stand,
Wishing to be found.

Part II: Summer Collection

The Fair in the Sky

Cotton candy in rows,
Keep the people on their toes.
Sunsets put on the best of show;
One of which everyone knows.
The big blue sky,
Wins first prize;
As well as the cherry pie.
My, oh my,
The people love the fair in the sky.

Cowboys and Cowgirls

We wear boots.
We can shoot.
We ride, with pride,
While sitting astride.
We wear hats and eat flapjacks.
We love big blue skies and burgers with fries.
We pledge allegiance to our God, then our flag.
We don't like to brag.
When the day ends,
We say prayers about our friends
and end them with an Amen.

Sunsets and Sunrises

Pink, purple, orange, and red,
All before I go to bed.
Blue clouds all around making it seem,
As if welcoming a king.
Peach, indigo, scarlet, and magenta,
All a part of my morning agenda.
All before the colors rise,
Early in the dawn before my eyes.
When all the colors try to set,
I will be watching yet.
The heavens rejoice, bursting in color,
All in praise of our creator.

The Three-Ring Circus

Welcome to the circus,
That is so very grand.
We have ponies, twirlers, tamers,
And we also have a band.
Watch that person jump so high,
Listen to the piano player's song.
Feel the clapping of the crowd,
The applause is so long.
You can buy cotton candy,
Hot dogs, or popcorn.
Enjoy yourself and have a good time,
Do not be so forlorn.
The ringmaster runs the show,
For he loves showing off.
The acrobat is doing flips,
No one dares to even cough.
Our show is amazing,
You should really come and see.
You will be stunned,
While shouting with glee.

Laugh

Sometimes it is good to laugh.
It may lead you down a good path.
Laughter is the greatest medicine of all.
It covers you like a shawl.
When your heart is broken,
Just find a joke to take the burden of that yoke.

Summer Days

The sun shines big and bright,
What a glorious sight.
Children are playing everywhere,
People are going to county fairs.
Ice cream cones and other treats,
Are really good things to eat.
Water sprinklers and swimming holes,
Watermelon in a bowl.
Climbing trees,
Getting skinned knees.
Lemonade stands,
Are very grand.
Riding bicycles,
And wishing for snow and icicles.
Sunsets of pink,
And parties at the skating rink.
These are the ways of summer days.

Part III:
Fall Collection

Pumpkin to Jack-o-Lantern

There are some round little things
growing in my yard.
They are very plump and have lots of funny bumps.
These things have an orange tint to them,
Almost as if to make people grin.
Oh, now I know these odd things,
They must be pumpkins.
My, they are quite a sight,
When I carve a face and add a light.
There is nothing spooky about these creatures,
Well, maybe just some of their features.

Who?

"Who?" calls the owl in the night, with
the moon shining oh so bright.
I asked the owl back,
"Who must you be talking to so late in the night?
You must remember to say goodnight."
"Who?" replies the owl,
so short and stout.
I really need to find who this owl is talking about.
My, oh my, see the creatures pass,
Right in front of your eyes of glass.
Still you must ask "Who?"
I think I found who you were talking to!

Teddy Bear

I cuddle with it every night,
For when mama turns out the light,
It gives me a bit of fright,
So I like to hold my teddy bear tight,
And then I know that everything
is going to be alright.

Shadows

Do you see that black thing on the wall?
It looks frightening and very tall.
It moves around in really weird ways;
I hope it decides to move away!
When I move,
It moves, as if trying to say,
"I can do what you do and I won't go away."
Oh wait,
Can this be?
The creature on the wall is really me?
Well that's not too bad,
Though it makes me sad.
I thought I had something really rad.
This shadow is really me and that's
the way it should be.

Autumn

Leaves fall,
From trees so tall.
Sun shines,
Oh so bright.
The breeze blows,
The river flows.
The birds fly,
Up so high.
Crunching leaves,
Make me believe this is autumn.

Part IV: Winter Collection

Telluride's Peak

You shall, you will, have to be meek,
To climb up Telluride's sunny peak.
When you get up to the top with the clouds,
You will say out loud,
"Oh what a beautiful place, surely
God's grace is upon my face."

Quilts and Things

Blankets and quilts and things,
All to keep you warm and cozy.
Full of stories told and untold.
Always there to warm you up,
And always good for a cup of tea.
Always there to keep you happy,
Even on the snowiest days.

A Starry Dream

The starry night sky,
Up so high,
With twinkling eyes,
That shine so bright.
Where the Milky Way flies
across a bridge of gloss.
On the other side,
A place full of shine,
Made so fine.
A planet made of clear glass,
A planet you could never surpass.
Up in that blanket of stars,
You dream and you will go far.

Titanic

Large and alone,
Riding the sea.
It is good to be out,
It is good to be free.
Narrow misses,
Then goodbye kisses.
Too large of a scrape to mend,
Nothing to do but abandon.
Everyone out of the queen,
For she will no longer be seen.
Underneath the ocean she goes,
The waters over her close.
Woe are the ones who rode that ship,
For it sunk so fairly quick.

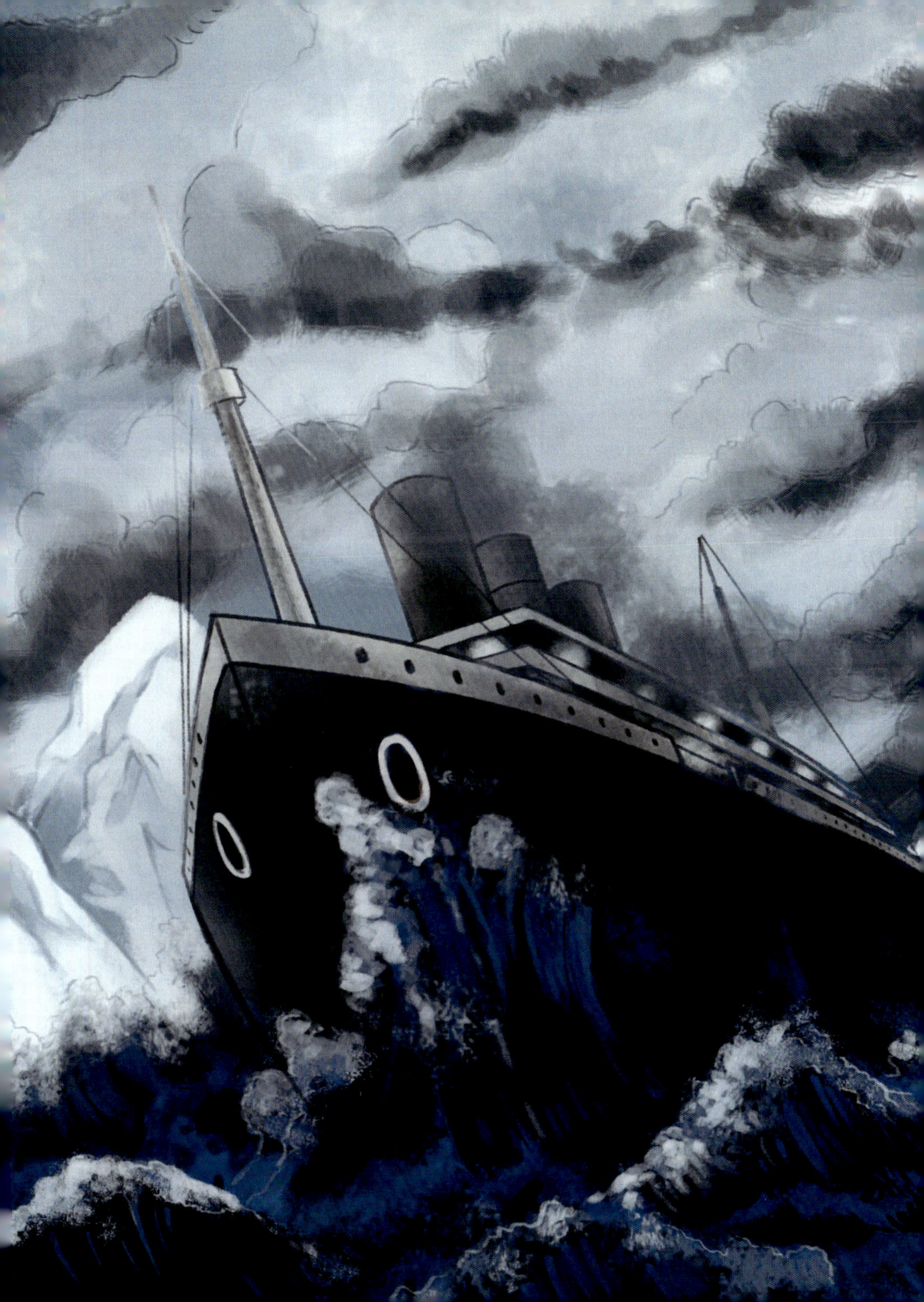

Part V: Miscellaneous

People

So many different people,
So many different places.
There are certain kinds of faces
that are hard to tell apart.
Others are very unique,
A work of God's great art.
They all act differently,
And believe in certain ways.
Do they know there are choices to make?
Many people like technology,
Reading, or sports,
Do they truly see it?
Do they just ignore?
You need eyes of wonder,
Some people say,
But do they really know,
Jesus is the way?

What Rhymes with Rhyme?

What rhymes with rhyme?
Might it be thyme or mime?
Could it be lime or slime?
What about climb or daytime?
Maybe it's I'm or dime?
One thing is for sure, there are a lifetime
of words that rhyme with rhyme.

The Private Investigator

Oh look out,
For he may be coming about.
Stay out of his way,
For he may be on a case.
Foiling robberies and chasing bad guys,
All apart of being a private I.
All those criminals,
Committing crimes,
If he is going to save the day,
Now would be the time.
Beware of this guy,
Because he is a private I.

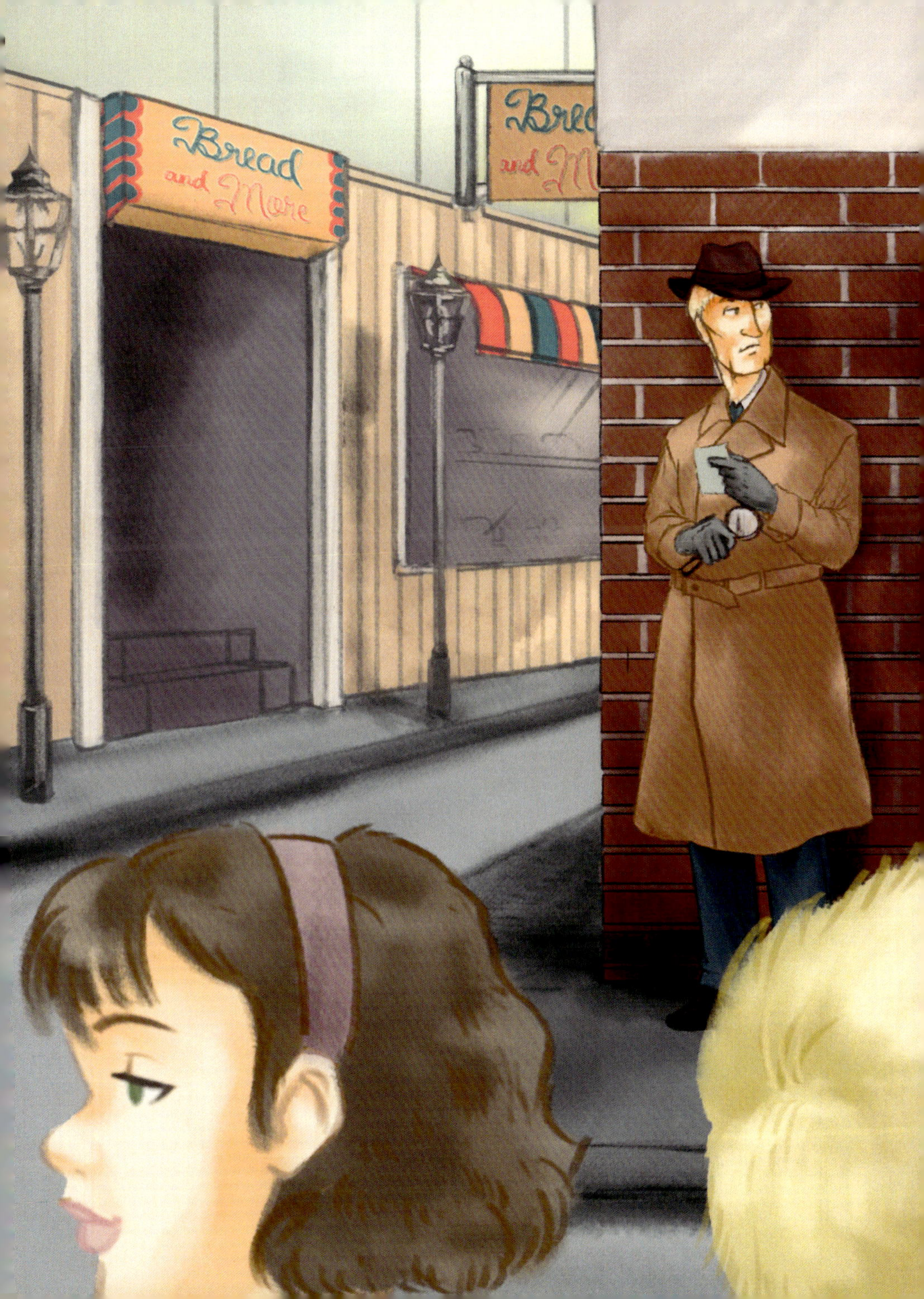
Bread
and More

The Potter

He shapes and kneads,
The clay will follow his lead.
He has an idea in his mind,
Every piece of pottery will be one of a kind.
He works day after day,
With hardly any pay.
The wheel spins round and round,
The clay is no longer in a mound.
His brow is furrowed in a crease.
His sturdy hands help form the
being of a masterpiece.

Biscuits

Biscuits and gravy,
Biscuits with honey,
All very good together.
Biscuits with butter,
Biscuits with jam,
All so fluffy and light.
Biscuits for supper,
Biscuits for dinner,
And biscuits for breakfast, too.
What a jolly good thing for biscuit
lovers like me and you!

The Child's Rhyme

Skip rope,
1, 2, 3,
Everyone shouts with glee.
Bounce the ball,
4, 5, 6,
Do a crazy trick.
Ride a bike,
7, 8, 9,
Everyone is doing just fine.
Climb a tree,
Number 10,
Somebody has a bruised shin.
Play hopscotch,

11, 12, 13,
Let's play kings and queens.
Go down the slide,
14, 15, 16,
There was a puddle at the bottom,
Now nobody is clean.
Play tag,
17, 18, 19,
Come on now, let's not be mean.
Duck, duck, goose,
Number 20,
I think I will stop now,
That is plenty!

Feet

I love the feeling
Of mud in my toes.
It is squishy and gushy,
And it only comes off with the hose.
I love the feeling
Of sand under my feet.
It feels warm and gritty
From the searing heat.
I love the feeling
Of grass underneath me.
It feels so smooth and plush,
And it is green as far as the eye can see.

e|LIVE

listen|imagine|view|experience

AUDIO BOOK DOWNLOAD INCLUDED WITH THIS BOOK!

In your hands you hold a complete digital entertainment package. In addition to the paper version, you receive a free download of the audio version of this book. Simply use the code listed below when visiting our website. Once downloaded to your computer, you can listen to the book through your computer's speakers, burn it to an audio CD or save the file to your portable music device (such as Apple's popular iPod) and listen on the go!

How to get your free audio book digital download:

1. Visit www.tatepublishing.com and click on the e|LIVE logo on the home page.
2. Enter the following coupon code:
   7c38-637d-c466-abe2-bc60-34b7-57f8-4f0d
3. Download the audio book from your e|LIVE digital locker and begin enjoying your new digital entertainment package today!